PUFFIN BOOKS

HANK PRANK AND HOT HENRIETTA

Life is anything but dull with H____ ____
getting into trouble, and his sister ____
the most terrible temper. Whereve____
holiday with their long-suffering ____
an outing – they seem to be set on causing trouble!

This is the first book by American author Jules Older.

Jules Older

Hank Prank and Hot Henrietta

Stories for Younger Children

Illustrated by
Lisa Kopper

PUFFIN BOOKS

Puffin Books, Penguin Books Ltd, Harmondsworth, Middlesex, England
Viking Penguin Inc., 40 West 23rd Street, New York, New York 10010, U.S.A.
Penguin Books Australia Ltd, Ringwood, Victoria, Australia
Penguin Books Canada Ltd, 2801 John Street, Markham, Ontario, Canada L3R 1B4
Penguin Books (N.Z.) Ltd, 182–190 Wairau Road, Auckland 10, New Zealand

First published by William Heinemann Ltd 1984
Published in Puffin Books 1987

Printed and bound in Great Britain by
Cox & Wyman Ltd, Reading

Contents

For the
first half
of the
fourth fastest
junior girls
relay team
in the South Island
of New Zealand

Amber and Willow

Hank Prank
and the Adenoids

Hank Prank wasn't Hank Prank's real name; Hank Prank's real name was Henry Bradley Lawes. But his mother and father called him Hank Prank and so did everyone else because Henry Bradley Lawes was always playing tricks and making jokes. When his mother said, "Henry, do you want a hamburger?" he'd answer, "I've never tasted a jamburger." Whenever Henry made a joke like that his mother would raise her eyebrows, roll her eyes, sigh deeply, and say, "Oh, Hank Prank!"

One day, when Hank had said 'potdogs' for 'hotdogs' and 'schmurtle' for 'turtle' and 'yucky' for 'lucky', Mrs Lawes turned to her husband and said, "Honey, I'm worried about Hank. I don't think he hears very well."

"He hears what he wants to," answered Hank's father, looking over the top of his newspaper.

"He's changed nearly every word I said to him today."

"That's his idea of a joke," said Mr Lawes. "That's why we call him Hank Prank."

"All the same, I'm going to take him to the doctor to have his ears checked."

The next morning Hank's mother made an appointment with the doctor. When they arrived at his office, the doctor said to Hank, "Hello Henry. I'm Dr Levy."

"Dr Sleevy?"

"No, Dr Levy."

"Dr Gravy?"

Hank's mother raised her eyebrows, rolled her eyes, sighed deeply, and muttered, "Oh, Hank Prank!"

Dr Levy examined Hank's throat, looked into his ears with a little light, and then gave him a hearing test. He took Hank into a small soundproof room, sat him in a swivel chair, and put real earphones on him. Hank liked that part. Then Dr Levy went out and spoke into a microphone outside the room. He told Hank to raise his hand whenever he heard a sound. Dr Levy and Hank could see each other through a window. Hank listened carefully for the sounds coming through the earphones, but he didn't hear many, and his hand usually stayed in his lap. After the hearing test Dr Levy called Hank out and said

to him, "Well, your mother's right, Hank. You do have a hearing problem."

"I have a steering problem? I'm not even old enough to drive!"

"You have a *hearing* problem, but we can cure it easily. You'll have to go to the hospital to have your adenoids out."

"I have to have my Dad in a doubt? Doubt about what?"

"No, no, Hank, adenoids. ADENOIDS! They're little lumps at the back of the throat,

9

and yours are a bit sore. When you have them out, you'll be able to hear again."

"I'm not allowed to drink beer now," Hank answered solemnly.

His mother and the doctor raised their eyebrows, rolled their eyes, sighed deeply, and together said, "Oh, Hank Prank!"

The hospital was in a city two hours away from where Hank and his family lived. Early one morning the Lawes family got up, had breakfast, and packed the car. With Mum and Dad in the front seat, and Hank and his sister Henrietta in the back, they left their home town and drove through the countryside towards the city. Henrietta fell asleep before they were out of town, but the rest of them were wide awake. Hank's mother said from the front seat, "Oh Hank, look at the billy goat."

"I don't see any silly boat," Hank answered.

Hank's mother sighed. A little later she pointed out the window and said, "Oh Hank, look at the pig farm."

Hank looked around and said, "A wigwam? There aren't any Indians around here, are there?" His father rolled his eyes. When they were almost at the hospital Hank's mother said, "Look at that big dog."

"What's a pig hog?" asked Hank. His father

and mother looked at each other and didn't say anything for a long time. Hank's father gripped the steering wheel tighter and muttered to himself. Finally, as they pulled into the driveway of the hospital, his father said very slowly and very quietly, "That operation had better work."

Inside the hospital they took an elevator to the children's ward. A young woman came out from behind a counter in the middle of the corridor and said, "Hello, I'm your nurse."

Hank answered, "You're not supposed to curse."

"Oh, you must be here for the adenoid operation," she went on. "It's being done by Dr Jones."

"By Dr Bones!" said Hank in a surprised voice. "What kind of a name is *that* for a doctor!"

"I'll take you to your room."

"I don't want a broom. I'm not going to sweep this place up. I'm here for an operation, you know."

His parents looked at each other a very long time, shook their heads sadly, and followed the nurse and Hank into the room. Hank's mother slept beside him in the room that night on a cot which the nurse brought in. He had a nice supper, but the next morning he was given no breakfast. The nurse told him that this was because today was the day he was going to have his operation. Soon after he got up, Hank's door opened and his father walked in. He sat on the bed and talked to Hank about hikes that the four of them were going to take when Hank was out of the hospital and back home, and he held Hank's hand. Then the door opened. A man wearing a white coat stepped inside.

"Hello, I'm Dr Jones."

"Hello, Dr Bones. I'm Hank Prank."

"Hello, Mr Spank. I'm Dr Bones."

"No, you're not. I am."

Dr Jones looked at Hank for a long time. "I think I see the way this conversation is going. Roll up your sleeve please."

Hank answered, "I don't have to sneeze."

"Your SLEEVE, Hank, your SLEEVE."

"Oh, my sleeve. What about my sleeve?"

"ROLL IT UP, PLEASE."

"Oh, roll it up. Why didn't you say so?"

By this time Dr Jones had reached down and rolled up Hank's sleeve himself. "Now, I'm going to give you a little needle," he said.

"A little tweedle?"

"Right, Hank. Here's your tweedle." And he stuck the tweedle in Hank's left arm.

"Ow!" said Hank. "That makes me very . . . very . . . uh . . . sleepy." He felt his eyes s-l-o-w-l-y closing.

Hank soon became sleepier and sleepier. He half remembered being lifted out of his bed and being put on a bed with wheels. He remembered riding on the bed down the hall, being pushed by another nurse with his father walking beside him and holding his hand. He didn't remember the operation at all. He thought he had a dream that he was in a room with doctors and nurses. One of them had put a little handkerchief over his mouth and nose. In the dream the handkerchief person said, "Now count to ten, Henry." Somebody with his voice counted, "One . . . two . . . three . . . four . . . snore . . ." He could remember no more.

When Hank woke up he was back in his own room in the hospital. His mother and father were both sitting on the bed next to him, and his father was holding his hand. Hank looked at him and then fell back to sleep.

When he woke up the next time, his parents were sitting in chairs beside the bed, and Henrietta was doing a puzzle on the floor. Hank's mother smiled at him. "HOW DO YOU FEEL, HANK?" she asked.

"Why are you shouting?" asked Hank.

"THE OPERATION'S OVER, HANK," said his father.

"Why are you two yelling?" asked Hank.

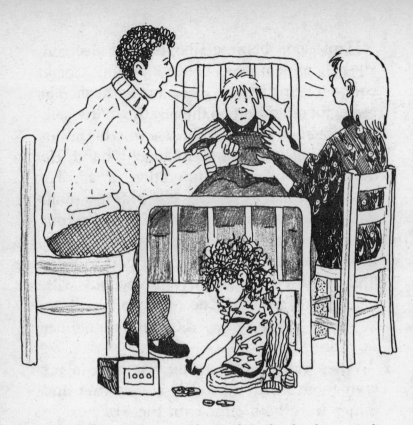

Then his father and mother looked at each other and smiled. The operation had worked. Hank could hear well again.

Hank smiled. Then he drifted back to sleep.

The next day the Lawes family left the hospital and drove back to their home. Hank sat in the back seat with a blanket across his lap to keep him warm. Henrietta slept again. After a while, Mrs Lawes looked out the window and said, "Look at that big dog."

Hank looked and answered, "Yes, it is a big dog." Hank's mother smiled.

A little later Hank's father pointed and said, "Hank, look at that pig farm." Hank looked and replied, "They sure have a lot of pigs there." Hank's father smiled.

As they got closer to home, both parents spoke at the same time, "Hank, look at the billy goat."

Hank waited a moment. Then he answered, "I don't see a silly boat!"

His parents looked at each other. Neither of them said a word. His father slowly stopped the car beside the road. They looked back at Hank. Their expressions were worried. But Hank had a big, silly grin on his face. "Fooled ya!" he said.

They looked at each other and laughed. Together they shook their heads, rolled their eyes, and sighed, "Oh, Hank Prank."

Hot Henrietta's First Day, Second Year

Hot Henrietta wasn't Hot Henrietta's real name. The Henrietta part was right. Both Henrietta and her brother's name, Henry, were traditional Lawes family names. The 'Hot' part came later. It had something to do with her temper.

But while she did get mad just a trifle faster than other people, there were some things and some people who always made her feel good all over. One of them was Mr Moss.

Henrietta had been at school for a year, and she was just crazy about her teacher, Mr Moss. He was her favourite person in the world. She planned to marry him. "Good old Mr Moss," she'd say as she drew yet another picture for him to pin on his bulletin board. She wrote letters to Mr Moss, and she wrote poems to Mr Moss. Hot tempered she might be, but Henrietta was just crazy about good old Mr Moss.

As the summer after her first year of school was ending, Henrietta could hardly wait for school to start again because then she'd see her old friend, Mr Moss. But on the last day of vacation, Henrietta's mother sat down next to her at the kitchen table and said, "Henrietta, I just got some news about your school."

"News! It *is* gonna start tomorrow, isn't it?" Henrietta loved school. Her brother Hank thought she was a little weird, but she did love school.

"It's about Mr Moss."

"Mr Moss! What's happening with Mr Moss? Is he coming to visit me?"

"Mr Moss is leaving."

"What?" Henrietta sat very still. "What did you say?"

"Mr Moss is leaving," her mother repeated. "He's going back to university to study some more."

"What do you mean, study some more? He's already clever enough."

"Henrietta, Mr Moss is going back to university. You have a new teacher. His name is Mr Price."

"Oh," said Henrietta. "His name is Mr Price. I have a new teacher, and his name is Mr Price. That's what you're telling me, isn't it, Mother? That I have a new teacher, and his name is Mr Price? Oh, very good. Very good.

Mr Moss isn't coming back, and Mr Price is. I feel sick."

"What do you mean, you feel sick, Henrietta? School starts tomorrow."

"I know that school is starting tomorrow. School is starting tomorrow without Henrietta. Henrietta is sick right now."

"How sick?"

"VERY sick, Mother. I have a sore throat, and a headache, and a stomach-ache. My arm hurts, and my other arm hurts. *Both* my legs hurt. I think I'm so sick I can never go to school again for the rest of my life. I don't want to go to school. I don't want to! I don't want to! You can't make me!"

"Henrietta, why don't you want to go to school?"

"Well, there's this new teacher. His name is Mr Price. I don't know him. But I have a feeling about him."

"What's your feeling, Henrietta?"

Henrietta's tears started down Henrietta's cheeks. "My feeling about this new teacher, Mr Price, is that he's horrible," she sobbed. "And he's big, and he's scary, and he hates kids, and he especially hates girls, and he's nowhere near as nice as Mr Moss. I don't want to go to school. And the other kids beat me up. I never told you that, but they do. And everybody's mean to me there, and I'm never going back. I'm sick. Please call a doctor."

"Oh, Henrietta," said her mother.

Into the kitchen walked Henrietta's father, carrying a basket of laundry from the line. "What's going on here?" he asked.

"I'm sick, Daddy. That's what's going on here. And your wife is going to send me to school anyway."

"Henrietta, what's the matter? You were fine a few minutes ago."

"Well, we've got a new teacher, and he's awful and he's scary. He's ugly, and he has horns and great fangy teeth. And I HATE him!"

"Henrietta, I didn't know you'd met your new teacher."

"Well, I haven't met him yet, but I have a bad feeling."

"Tell you what," said her father. "Tomorrow, when we go to school for the first day, I'll go in with you, and we'll meet this monster together. What's his name?"

"Price," said Henrietta. "Price is his name, and Price is a name I don't like."

The next day, Henrietta and her Daddy went to school together. Well, that's not quite right. Mr Lawes went to school. Henrietta disappeared somewhere between the car and the school door. He thought she was right beside him. They'd got out of the car together. They'd started down the path together. They were right next to each other, when all of a sudden Henrietta disappeared. Mr Lawes was already in the school when he looked down for Henrietta and couldn't find her. He walked back as far as the parking lot, and there she was, hiding behind a fender of a Ford Escort.

"Henrietta, is something the matter?"

"I know what it's going to be like in there.

The other kids are going to beat me up. This new teacher is going to hate me. And besides, I've forgotten my book. I can't go to school without my library book."

"Henrietta, the library hasn't even opened!"

"It's from last year. I never told you this, Daddy, but I've had a library book all summer. Can we go home and get it now? I think I know where it is."

"Sorry, Henrietta. The bell's about to ring."

Together they walked into school. But that's not quite right either. Mr Lawes walked into school. Henrietta was more or less dragged into school. Well, she wasn't exactly dragged into school, but her heels were leaving long black skid marks on the pavement. She wasn't exactly crying, but she wasn't exactly not crying. She was sort of snorfulling.

As soon as they were in the classroom door, she rushed into a corner and looked around. She was looking for someone big, and scary, with horns and fangs, and bright red hair that stood straight up.

She couldn't find him.

But there, sitting at the piano, was somebody playing a very pleasant tune. She didn't recognise him, but she didn't trust him either. Why should she? He wasn't Mr Moss.

He continued to play this pleasant tune,
and a lot of kids were hanging around the
piano humming and singing the same tune.

Some of the kids came over and said, "Hi,
Henrietta. What have you been doing all
summer?"

Nobody actually beat her up, and she
couldn't help but notice that her headache
was rapidly going away. She got one step
closer to the piano. The tune continued, but
the man at the piano looked over at her, and
said, "Hello. Are you Henrietta? The other

kids were telling me about you." The whole time he continued to play.

She moved one step closer to the piano, and motioned to her Daddy to come along beside her.

"Why don't you join the group?" the piano man asked. "We're just singing a very nice song."

She moved one step closer to the piano. Her Daddy moved with her. She looked at him, and she looked at Mr Price. She looked back at her Dad, and she looked at the other kids. She looked back at her father.

"Yes, Henrietta?" he asked.

"Well, I couldn't help but wonder, Father, just what you're doing here. You know it embarrasses me when you come to school. Would you mind leaving now? We're about to start our song."

And with that he tiptoed out the door.

Teeth and the Teacher

Hank Prank lost his two top front teeth. It was an unfortunate time to lose them, really, because just when he was without these small but important parts of his body, Miss Sissons was teaching the class how to pronounce the letter 's'.

"Quite ssimply," she said, putting great emphasis on the 's', "it'ss like thiss. We pronounce the letter 's' ass followss: 'Ssilly Ssammy ssaw Ssuzy ssmiling.' Now classs, you ssay it after me."

And everyone repeated, "Silly Sammy saw Suzy smiling." That is, everybody but one. Hank Prank. He said it like this: "Thilly Thammy thaw Thuthy thmiling."

In a sugar-sweet voice Miss Sissons spoke to her students. "That was very good, children, very good indeed." In a slightly less sweet voice, she then said, "Hank, come here."

Hank pushed his chair back from his desk

and marched to the front of the room. Miss Sissons knelt beside him. "Say after me, Hank, 'Ssilly Ssammy ssaw Ssuzy ssmiling'."

Hank repeated after her, "Thilly Thammy thaw Thuthy thmiling."

Miss Sissons looked at Hank from the top of his head to the laces on his shoes. After a long while, she said, "Open your mouth, Hank."

"Aaaaahh," was the sound that automatically poured out of Hank's mouth when anybody asked him open it.

"Show us your teeth, Hank."

"Eeeeehh," was the sound of Hank's teeth being shown.

"Hank, there's something missing in your mouth, isn't there?"

"What'th mithing?" he asked.

"Well Hank, it's like this. You've lost your two front teeth."

Hank laughed, "Ha, ha. I've lotht my two front teeth." He laughed again. "Ha, ha. I've lotht my two front teeth." Then he cried, "Waaa! My teeth are mithing!"

"What's the matter, Hank?"

"My Dad'll kill me. Oh, where could I have lotht them? Yethterday I lotht my watch, today I've lotht my two front teeth. What will they thay? Oh, they'll be tho mad!"

"Hank, Hank. Hey, Hank! Relax. Hank, stop crying. HANK!"

"I'm not crying," he snorfulled. "I'm not crying. I don't cry. I never cry."

"Hank," Miss Sissons explained, "Hank, you haven't lost them like you lost your watch. And by the way, your watch turned up in 'Lost and Found' today. You can take it home with you tonight. Hank, you haven't *lost* your teeth. They just fell out."

"Oh," he said. "Oh, they jutht fell out. WAAA!"

"Hank, Hank," she said, putting her arm around him. "Stop crying!"

"I'm not crying. My teeth fell out. And you tell me not to cry. What am I going to do without teeth? How am I going to eat thteak? I'm going to be tho embarrathed for the retht of my life."

"No, no, Hank. You've lost your *baby* teeth. You're going to have *big* teeth grow in where they were."

"Oh, *big* teeth," he replied, thinking carefully. "How big?"

"Normal-sized teeth, like mine," and she smiled broadly at him.

Miss Sissons actually had very big teeth—*very* big teeth—and Hank wasn't entirely sure this was just what he wanted.

But he stopped not-crying and snorfulling long enough to say, "Well, that'th very good, but what'th the matter with the way I thaid that thententh?"

"Which thententh, Hank? I mean, which *ssentence*, Hank?"

"That thententh that you thaid. Thilly Thammy thaw Thuthy thmiling. I thaid it jutht like the other kidth. I thaid it jutht thplendidly, but you call me up here and tell me my teeth are falling out!"

"Well, Hank," Miss Sissons replied, "you didn't actually say it just like I did. Because I said it like this: Sssilly Sssammy sssaw Sssuzy sssmiling."

Her 's's were now so sibilant that a glass of water which was sitting on the piano, suddenly cracked.

Hank looked exasperated. "That'th what I thaid: Thmiling Thuthy thaw thilly Thammy thmiling. Oh, now I've got it all mixtht up!"

Miss Sissons put her chubby arm around Hank's shoulder. "Hank, don't you worry about a thing. Inthide of thixth—inside of six months, you're going to have brand-new teeth, and you'll be able to say all your words jusst like I."

"Jutht like me," Hank answered.

"Just like I," she answered back.

"Jutht like *me*," he said again. And he added, "You thaid, 'jutht like I', but you *meant*, 'jutht like me'."

She couldn't remember what the rule was for that sentence, so she just said what everyone says in this kind of situation: "Oh, Hank Prank!"

Then he put his little arm around *her* shoulder. "Be throng, Mith Thithonth. You'll get it right the nextht time."

Hands Up Who Doesn't Like Henrietta!

One very usual day, Henrietta left her house as usual, crossed Ravensbourne Road as usual, and walked up the hill to school as usual. All her friends were there as usual. Everyone was talking all at the same time as usual. But this day something *un*usual happened.

When Henrietta started to ask her friend Jane what she was drawing, Jane said crossly, "Oh, I'm tired of you, Henrietta." And when she walked over to where her friend Rob was building a model lighthouse, Rob didn't even look up. "I'm busy, Henrietta. Don't bother me now."

Henrietta's stomach began to feel very heavy, as if there was a small pumpkin sitting in it. She slowly dragged herself over to her friend Rangi. But Rangi had just lost a fight and was trying not to cry. When she said hello, he just shook his head from side to side.

Henrietta's small pumpkin turned into a fat watermelon. She shuffled over to Marjorie, who was a little bit older than the other kids and who should have known better. "Marjorie, nobody seems to like me today."

Marjorie had been arguing with her bratty brother all morning. She snapped at Henrietta, "Well, neither do I." Then she turned to the class, and in a loud voice, commanded, "Hands up who doesn't like Henrietta!"

Nearly the whole class put their hands up. Henrietta felt just terrible. Her watermelon turned to lead. There's nothing that feels worse than having a whole class put their hands up to say they don't like you.

Now, she knew that a lot of people whose

hands were up were people who did like her, and she knew that they were just putting their hands up because Marjorie said to. But it didn't make her feel any better. She felt awful, so awful she couldn't even get mad. Henrietta looked through a plump tear in each eye, and she saw that every hand in the room was up except one.

The one hand that wasn't raised belonged to the newest girl in the class. Her name was Tania. Tania looked at all the raised hands, but her hand stayed down. Then she looked at Marjorie. Marjorie, whose hand wasn't only up but was waving like a flag, glared at Tania. But still Tania's hand stayed on the desk top.

Besides being the newest child in the class, Tania was the littlest. When she sat at her desk, her feet didn't even reach the floor. But now she carefully pushed her desk aside, slid off her chair, and walked across the room to where Henrietta stood with a tear working its way down each cheek. Tania put her little arm around Henrietta's waist, and in a voice just loud enough for everyone to hear, said, "I like Henrietta."

Right away Rangi spoke up. "Well, I like Henrietta too."

"So do I!" shouted Rob and Jane at the same time.

Marjorie jumped to her feet. "Whose idea was this, anyway? I like Henrietta." Her hand came to rest in her lap.

Nobody dared say whose idea it was, but as soon as Marjorie's hand went down, everybody else's did too.

That night when Henrietta and Hank and their mother and father were eating dinner, she told them about what had happened. Her parents looked first at each other and then at her. Then Henrietta's father quietly asked, "What was the most important thing about what happened today?"

Henrietta thought for a minute and then answered. "Well, I felt terrible when everybody said they didn't like me, even though I really knew they did like me. That was important. And I saw the way all the other kids put up their hands when Marjorie put hers up, and that was important. But I guess the most important thing was when Tania didn't put up her hand, and when she came over and put her arm around me. That made me feel good."

Henrietta picked up her fork, carefully cut a potato into four pieces, and lifted one of them towards her mouth. But before it got past her chin, she stopped, thought a moment, and put it back on her plate. "Maybe the most, *most* important thing was that as soon as she did it, the other kids followed her, and then they said that they liked me too."

After a long pause Henrietta's mother spoke. "I guess you can be a leader even when you're little. And you can be a leader when you're helping people, and not hurting them."

"I think I'll go to bed now," said Henrietta, quietly. "Goodnight."

"Goodnight," said her father.

"Goodnight," said her mother.

"'Night, Henrietta," said Hank.

Hot Henrietta Cools Off

One snowy winter's morning, Hot Henrietta and her brother Hank had a big fight which ended with Hank breaking her favourite aeroplane. When she went to her mother with the broken plane, Mrs Lawes didn't want to hear about it. "You're too old to be fighting anyway," was all she said.

So she charged into the kitchen to tell her father about how mean his wife was acting. But all he had to say was, "Stop complaining about your mother, Henrietta."

She slammed the door as she left for school to tell the principal what a terrible family she had. But when she whipped into his office, Mr Dunn was working his way through a huge stack of papers, and all he said was, "Where's that library book you were supposed to bring back today?"

Henrietta stormed out of the principal's office and into her classroom. She started to tell her friends what a rat Mr Dunn was, but they weren't interested. Their only comment was, "Sorry Henrietta, we're busy drawing right now."

Well, *that* was the end. Henrietta stomped her foot once, very hard, marched out the door, and left the lot of them gaping at her back. That's right—she walked right out of school. She *stormed* out of school! Her ears were smoking when she walked out that door.

It wasn't her fault that she had an awful, nasty, evil, brother, and a cruel, uncaring mother, and a father who never understood her, and a terrible school principal whose only interest was in late library books, and the worst friends in the world. It wasn't her fault, but she didn't have to put up with it either. No Sir! And as she stomped along the street, her feet were so hot that her footprints melted the snow.

"I don't have to put up with that," she muttered to herself. "I'm not GOING to put up with that! There's no REASON I have to put up with that. I'm not going to put up with THAT!"

She clomped up the steps, and the wood charred under her feet. She opened the door, and the door handle came off in her hand. Nobody was home. She slammed the door, and two pictures fell off the wall. She

35

clambered up the stairs, and the carpet on them smouldered. She kicked open the door to her room, and she pulled a big suitcase from under the bed.

"Huh," she said to her koala bear, "I don't have to put up with school any more. I don't have to put up with this family any more. I don't have to put up with *anything* any more! I'm going skiing."

And as she spoke, the light snow which had been falling came down a little bit heavier, as if even it were afraid of Hot Henrietta when she was really angry. Right now, she was really angry.

"Now, what shall I pack?" she wondered, pulling the drawers out of her bureau one by one and throwing them on the floor.

"Oh, a glove. One bloomin' glove. Swell. Oh, here's one pair of underpants. Marvellous. Here's a ski. Oh, terrific. One ski. Oh grand!" She threw that in the suitcase too. It didn't fit. She tossed it on the floor.

She packed a few small items: two jars of peanut butter, three Chock Bars, four more Chock Bars, a carrot, skis (she found the other one), poles and boots. One ice skate. (She hadn't found the other one.) A glove, a mitten, another mitten, her other glove, and just in case she got cold, a scarf which she wrapped around her neck. Then she found the other ice skate and put it on the floor next to its mate.

That should do it, she thought. But she took a few comic books from her brother Hank, just to show him that he couldn't break her aeroplane and get away with it.

Everything went in the suitcase except the ski gear, the gloves, and the mittens. She looked around one last time and noticed her sunglasses in one of the drawers that was lying on the floor. She put them on.

Henrietta snapped shut the tightly-packed suitcase and dragged it down the still-smouldering stairs. Then she climbed back upstairs, grabbed her skis and boots and poles, and thumped them down the stairs. She put on her boots and hoisted her skis and poles over her shoulder. With her other hand she lifted her suitcase, decided it was too heavy to carry, and left it by the front door. Then she marched out of the house and up the street towards the top of Ravensbourne Hill.

By now the snow was falling heavily. But she trudged through it: up, and up, and up the hill. Past the school. Past the Play Centre. Past her friends' houses. Right up through the bush, until she was standing at the very top of the steep and dangerous Ravensbourne Hill.

Was she scared? Not a bit. Was she mad?

And how! She was burning. "I'll show 'em!" Henrietta laid her skis in the snow pointing straight down the hill. She put her boots into her skis, and snapped them in. She put on her gloves, and over her gloves she put on her mittens, just in case she got cold.

Snapped into her skis, Henrietta gazed down the long, steep hill.

First there was the bush, all covered with snow. Then a few houses, some with wisps of smoke hanging around their chimneys. Next came the Play Centre, then Henrietta's school, and across the road some more houses, including her own. And then, at the bottom of the hill, Henrietta could see and hear heavy trucks rumbling along Harbour Road which ran across the bottom of Ravensbourne. The only thing beyond Harbour Road was a steep drop into the harbour. There were sharks in the harbour.

Was Henrietta scared? Not even a little. She adjusted her sunglasses. She grabbed her poles. She kicked with her left foot, and she began to ski straight down the hill.

Faster and faster she went. Through the bush—straight through it, ploughing up trees and bushes and flax. Now she was skiing past the Play Centre where the little kids went, "Ooh, Mummy! Look! What 'dat?"

Henrietta shot past her own school, past

her friends building a snowman in the playground. Their heads corkscrewed—"What the heck was *that*?" Mr Dunn had just finished arranging all the library cards and was carefully carrying them to the library when he glanced out his office window. "What on earth was that?" he asked himself. When he figured out, not what, but *who* it was, his jaw dropped and so did every one of the cards.

Henrietta flew past her own house. Her mother was home by now, and she called, "Henriettaaaaaaaa" as her daughter whizzed by. Henrietta never even waved.

Still faster she skied; by now she was going at least a million miles an hour and picking up speed all the time. Just seconds in front of her lay the dangerous Harbour Road.

An enormous truck was roaring along the road from the left, and an even more enormous truck was thundering along from the right. Henrietta was heading straight between them! What could she do?

(Before I tell you what she did, think about what you'd do if you were skiing along at over a million miles an hour and an enormous truck was coming at you from the left and an even more enormous truck was bearing down on you from the right, *and* neither driver even saw you because they were both so busy talking to each other on their CB radios.)

Here's what Henrietta did. She crouched down and skied even faster! She s-q-u-e-e-z-e-d through the tiny sliver of a crack that separated those two trucks. The drivers, who were still talking to each other on their CB radios, called out, "Ten-four! Ten-four! Eleven-fifteenths! Mayday! What was that? Great Smokey Bear! What *was* that? Over and o-u-t!"

She'd made it across the road, but now Henrietta was faced with something even worse. For just one inch in front of her loomed the steep drop into the harbour. There were sharks in the harbour.

What could she do? She was racing at two million miles an hour on skis, on slippery snow, and had only one inch to go before she reached a cliff. At the bottom of the cliff the cold water of the harbour waited for her. There were sharks in the harbour.

What could she do? What would *you* do? *She* did the only thing she could do. She did what you would have done under these difficult circumstances. Henrietta executed a perfect parallel stop. She stopped her skis half of a half of a mouse's nose from the drop to the icy water. She stopped so short that her skis kicked two tons of snow into the harbour. It

landed with such a splash that the sharks swam away in a hurry.

Then she took off her skis, placed them over her shoulder, looked both ways before crossing the road, walked straight up to her house, leaned her skis against the front porch, ignored her mother who was standing there on the porch with her mouth still open, marched back up the hill to school, dusted the snow off her mittens, removed the mittens with her teeth, took off her gloves one finger at a time, let each glove flutter to the floor, and, to the amazement of Mr Dunn and her friends, sat down at her desk, placed her sunglasses on the desk, opened her book, and in the most polite and refined voice any of them had ever heard, said, "So now we may perhaps begin. Yes?"

Now Hank Takes Off

Henrietta wasn't the only one to leave home. Some time later, her adorable brother Hank did the same thing. This time the problem was piano lessons.

It wasn't just that Hank hated the piano (which he did). It wasn't that he hated being stuck inside the house every Wednesday afternoon after school (which he did). It wasn't that he had no talent at all for playing the piano (which he didn't). The problem was the piano teacher.

The piano teacher who taught Hank and his neighbour Alistair (Goody - Goody) Llewellyn-Jones every Wednesday afternoon was one Percival Sanwich. Percival Sanwich had two bad habits, both of which were driving Hank out of his mind. One was that whenever his students made a mistake he rapped them sharply over the knuckles with a six-inch ruler which he usually used for keeping time. This was bad enough, but the second habit was even worse. For lunch Percival Sanwich invariably ate raw garlic sandwiches, and when he leaned over on the bench and said to Hank, "Hhhow are you today, Hhhaaank?" the poor lad almost fainted.

One Wednesday morning Hank announced at the breakfast table that he was not going to go to piano lessons that afternoon or any other afternoon.

"What did you say?" asked his father, looking over the top of his paper.

"I said," said Hank, "that I, Henry Bradley Lawes, also known as Hank Prank, am no longer going to piano lessons as long as I live, so help me God."

"That's what I thought you said," answered his father. "And I want to inform you that I, Marc Lawes, also known as your father, insist that you *are* going to piano lessons both this afternoon and for as long as I tell you you're going to piano lessons!"

Hank went to piano lessons. But that afternoon, Percival Sanwich smelled like he'd eaten a double dose of garlic and gave Hank no less than six raps with the ruler.

The next Wednesday morning Hank had another breakfast announcement to make. This one he said more quietly but with considerably more determination in his voice.

"I'm not going to music any more."

His father again looked over the top of his paper, but before he could speak Hank's mother said, "I thought we'd been through this last week."

His father chimed in, "Right. We *have* been through this last week."

Hank spoke into his cereal bowl, never raising his eyes above the rim. "Last week," he said in slow, quietly dramatic tones. "Last week was just practice for this week." Hank could feel two hot spots like heat lamps pointed his way. One glowed from where his father sat, and the other, from where his mother stood.

Together they said, "Now you listen to me, Young Man—" then looked at each other, in surprise. Hank's father continued, "You *are* going to your piano lessons, and you *will* practise your piano, and we will *not* discuss it any further. Do you understand?"

Hank murmured something into his bowl.

"I heard that. What was it?" his father stated and asked in the same breath.

Hank didn't answer but pushed himself away from the table, collected his books, and set out for school.

On Wednesday afternoons, Hank came home from school, had a quick snack, and either got in the car with his mother to pick up Goody-Goody Alistair or else waited outside until Mrs Llewellyn-Jones picked him up. Whoever was driving, the destination was always the same—piano lessons. This particular Wednesday it was Mrs Llewellyn-Jones' turn.

Hank came home, but for once he didn't go right to the refrigerator. This Wednesday he marched up to his mother who was sitting at the kitchen table drawing designs for a stained glass lamp. Instead of giving her a hug, Hank stood at attention three feet from her chair.

"What's the matter, Hank?" she asked.

"There is nothing the matter, Mother, except that I am not going to piano today. Or any other day."

Mrs Lawes had forgotten the breakfast conversation, but now that she was reminded of it, her anger came flashing back. In her firmest voice she commanded, "Oh yes you are going. And since you're marching, my little soldier, you can about-face and march right outside and wait for Mrs L-J who will be arriving momentarily. Dismissed!"

Hank turned on his heel and marched out of the kitchen, marched down the hall, marched out the front door and down the steps, and marched through the gate. There

he turned right and just kept on marching.
That boy marched, and he marched, and he
marched. Hank Prank wasn't *running* away
from home, he was *marching* away.

Meanwhile back at the house, Mrs
Llewellyn-Jones and the dreaded Alistair
pulled up outside the gate. When she didn't
see Horrid Henry (as she privately called
him), Mrs L-J discreetly honked her horn,
then waited a few moments and honked
again, this time a little longer. The third blast
from her horn was considerably longer and
brought Mrs Lawes down to the gate.

"Hello, Mrs Llewellyn-Jones," she said.
"Hello, Alistair."

"Good afternoon, my dear. And where, might one ask, is your delightful son, Henry?"

"My delightful son Hen . . . You mean he isn't . . . I guess he's . . . Mrs Llewellyn-Jones, I think you'd better go on without him today. Please tell Mr Sanwich that my delightful son Henry is unable to attend." Without another word she whirled and, as her son had done moments before in the opposite direction, marched through the gate.

And she continued to march, or rather to pace, once she was inside the front door. As she trudged down the hallway carpet towards the kitchen her fury grew.

"I'll murder that kid. I'll spank him till he's black and blue and green and yellow. I'll show *him* who's boss around here!"

But as she made her turn by the kitchen door and headed towards the front, her anger turned to worry.

"What if something's happened to him? My dear little Henry. He's not a bad boy, just . . ."

By this time she'd made her second turn, and with her change of direction came a change of heart. "Whatever happens he deserves. Imagine making his mother suffer like this. And the humiliation in front of that horrible Mrs . . ."

By this time she'd made her turn again. "Oh, I'm so glad he's not like that awful Alistair. I couldn't stand a child who obeyed everything I said. Suppose he's been abducted. Suppose someone's lured him into a car or . . ." She reached the front door, rounded the turn, and changed tack again.

"If anyone was dumb enough to kidnap Hank, within two hours they'd be begging me to take him back. It would be the first case in history of a reverse ransom, and I'd make 'em pay plenty. I'll make *him* pay too when he gets home!"

The kitchen door again. At the word 'home', tears started to run down her cheeks as she thought about her darling little boy, lost and alone in a strange and frightening world.

Meanwhile, on his Long March, Hank was also going through some changes. For the first four blocks he was full of anger and resentment. The meanest parents in the world! I'd rather live anywhere but there. I'd rather be dead than live with them, and if I died, wouldn't they be sorry! They'd know it was all their fault. They drove me to it, them and old Garlic Breath.

Hank pictured his parents wailing mournfully at his funeral while all their neighbours and relations pointed accusing fingers at them. He studied the picture and enjoyed it.

But as Hank marched along (now a little slower than before) he began to dwell less on the funeral and more on the fact that he'd be the only person at the funeral who was dead. This had a somewhat chilling effect on young Henry, and his mood slowly changed from anger to sorrow. No more baseball, no more friends, no more sleeping in his own bed. Being dead began to have less and less appeal. Hank's steps grew even slower, and when he came to the next corner he turned round, and without really meaning to, began to head in the general direction of . . . home.

He couldn't stop thinking of the things he'd have to give up if he died, and each one felt like another ten pound weight on his little shoulders. No more watermelon. No more Mom's chocolate cake with caramel icing. No more Mom! Hank began to speed up. By the time he'd reached his own block, he was running. He burst through the gate and dashed up the walk towards the front door.

Meanwhile, back inside, Mrs Lawes' pacing had worn a path in the carpet like a trail through a grassy meadow. Now she couldn't stay angry even on her trips towards the kitchen, and she thought more and more about what terrible harm had befallen her boy. On her final kitchen patrol she decided that she had to do something. On her last turn she decided that her pacing had to come to an end. And as she headed for the door with quickening steps, she decided that she had to go out and find her son.

That decision made her feel instantly better, and by the time she reached the door she was practically running. She turned the handle and *pulled*.

At that very moment, Hank arrived, fairly flying up the porch steps, and grabbed the door handle. With both hands he pressed down the latch and *pushed*.

Hank's push and his mother's pull came at exactly the same time. The front door swung

open as though a bull had charged through it. An extremely surprised Mrs Lawes was flung backwards halfway down the hallway, and an even more surprised Hank now really flew. He sailed through the air with the most amazed look on his face as his mother careered into the well-worn carpet. But his flight was a short one, and his landing, none too smooth. Hank's head landed with a whoosh on his mother's stomach.

"Oooff!" was the sound Mrs Lawes made.

"Woooff!" was the sound Hank made.

Both of them were too stunned and too winded to speak. First they looked around to see where they were. Then they looked at the open door to try and figure out how they got there. Finally they looked at each other. They looked for a long time. Then they started to laugh.

Hank tried to get up, but he was laughing too hard, and he fell back down on to his mother. Mrs Lawes tried to sit up, but she was laughing so hard that she rolled back on to the carpet. They laughed until they cried. Then they cried until they laughed. In the end they couldn't tell whether they were laughing or crying, but they knew they were glad to be back together at home.

Temper, Temper . . .

One day Henrietta's temper proved too great even for Mrs Kapa, her teacher, who was the very picture of patience.

"Henrietta," she said, "I'm the very picture of patience, but your temper has proved too great even for me."

Henrietta glared up from her desk, "I didn't do nuffin'."

"Henrietta, I didn't do *anything*."

"I never said you did."

Mrs Kapa looked confused. "Never said I did what, Henrietta?"

"I never said you did anything. It's you who's been pickin' on me all day."

"Henrietta, that's the last straw."

"I don't care!"

"You're going to write, 'I will not lose my temper in class', five hundred times."

"I WON'T!"

"You won't what, Henrietta?" Mrs Kapa

suddenly looked very big and scary as she loomed over Henrietta's desk.

"I . . . WON'T . . . lose my temper in class, Mrs Kapa."

"Indeed, you won't, my girl. And I want 500 lines to that effect by tomorrow morning."

Henrietta stopped talking, but she didn't stop thinking. It's not fair, she thought. It's not fair at all. So what if I have a bad temper. Toby's rude, but Mrs Kapa doesn't make him write, "I won't be rude in class". Laura has red hair, but she doesn't have to write, "I won't be a redhead in class". Well, I've got a temper. But I'm not gonna write any 500 lines about it. It's just not fair.

Henrietta kept on thinking, and by three o'clock, Henrietta had a plan. As soon as the bell rang, she ran out of class and down the hall to the front door. When the other kids came tumbling out of their classrooms and spilling out the door, she hauled out her friends as they passed. First Laura, then Toby and Sandeep, and finally Natalie and Ben. When she had them all assembled, here's what she said:

"Look you guys, we've got a problem. Mrs Kapa told me I had to write 500 lines by tomorrow morning."

"Then why do *we* have a problem?" Toby wanted to know.

"Because *we* know it's not fair that *I* have to write 500 lines."

"You probably deserved it," Toby answered. He liked Mrs Kapa a lot.

"You shut up, Toby," Henrietta snapped back. "I need your help. Five hundred lines is a lot, but if we each write 100, I could hand them in tomorrow, and she'd never know the difference. So we each go home and write 100 times, 'I will not lose my temper in class'."

Toby piped up again. "Wait a minute. There's five of us, not counting you, Henrietta. If all of us do 100 lines, then you don't have to do any. Besides, you probably deserved it—so count me out!"

Henrietta glared at him as he ran off, but the others stayed and copied down the sentence. They all agreed to deliver 100 lines apiece to Henrietta before 9 o'clock the next morning.

That night Henrietta wrote "I will not lose my temper in class", one hundred times in her exercise book, then carefully tore the page out of the book. She went to bed chuckling about how clever she was.

The next morning she got up early and waited for her friends just outside the school door. They straggled into school, one by one.

Sandeep was the first to arrive. He handed her his 100 lines carefully written on exercise

paper with black ink. Then Laura rode up on
her bike and gave Henrietta 100 lines written
on a writing pad with blue ink. Ben's 100 lines
were on school paper like Henrietta's, but he
scribbled them in pencil. Natalie's contribu-
tion was beautifully printed on Holly Hobby
stationery. All her 'i's were dotted with
hearts.

Henrietta handed all five pages to Mrs
Kapa. Mrs Kapa looked at Henrietta's page
and smiled. Then Mrs Kapa looked at Sandeep's page and smiled a little less. Then Mrs

Kapa looked at Ben's page with puzzled eyes. Then Mrs Kapa considered Laura's page. And finally, Mrs Kapa carefully examined Natalie's page with all the 'i's dotted with hearts.

"Henrietta," she sighed, "did you do all these lines yourself?"

Henrietta's temper ripped into top gear. "You never said I had to do them myself. You just said I had to GET THEM DONE!"

"Oh," replied Mrs Kapa calmly. "Well, perhaps I didn't specify that you were to do them yourself, Henrietta. I'm so sorry. Tonight you can write 500 more lines, and this time, please do them yourself."

Henrietta was about to hit the roof when she noticed that Mrs Kapa was looking unnaturally calm. She looked the kind of calm teachers look before they blow up and yell for the principal and start throwing erasers around the room. Henrietta said nothing.

But Henrietta kept on thinking. After school that day, Henrietta went straight home to her parents' desk. She knew just what she was looking for. She opened the stationery drawer and pulled out nine pieces of paper. Five of them were white typing paper and four were black carbon paper. She laid one white sheet on the desk and placed one black sheet of carbon paper neatly on top of it. On top of that she put one more piece of white, and on top of that, one more piece of carbon. When they were all carefully stacked and a fresh, clean sheet of white paper rested on the top as well as the bottom, Henrietta took out a ballpoint pen. As hard as she could, she wrote on the top sheet, "I will not lose my temper in class." She wrote it one hundred times. Then she carefully lifted the four sheets of carbon paper from the pile. On every white sheet the words, "I will not lose my temper in class" appeared one hundred times. Henrietta looked very satisfied with herself. "Hummph," she muttered, "hot-tempered I may be, but dumb I'm not."

Next morning Henrietta handed Mrs Kapa the five sheets of paper, each with the same sentence written one hundred times.

"This time I did them myself!"

Mrs Kapa looked at the first sheet and smiled. Mrs Kapa then looked at the second sheet and smiled a little less. Mrs Kapa looked at the third sheet with puzzled eyes. Mrs Kapa frowned as she studied the fourth sheet. When she examined the fifth sheet, Mrs Kapa grew very quiet. "Henrietta," she said at last, "I don't think you wrote these yourself."

Henrietta's temper shot up like a rocket. "I didn't say I *wrote* them myself! I said I *did* them myself. That's what you told me to do, AND THAT'S WHAT I DID!"

"Henrietta, what was that sentence I gave you to wri— to do?"

"I WILL NOT LOSE MY TEMPER IN CLASS!"

"And what are you doing now, Henrietta?"

"I AM NOT LOSING MY . . ."

"Yes, Henrietta, you are not losing your . . .?"

Now a puzzled look crept into *Henrietta's* eyes.

Mrs Kapa smiled. "Henrietta," she said, "if I told you to do those 500 lines again tonight, I suppose you'd photocopy them."

"Well . . ."

"Well, what, Henrietta?"

"Well," Henrietta answered slowly, "there's a Xerox machine where my Dad works . . ."

"And if I said to do them again tomorrow night?"

Henrietta smiled. "Sandeep has a computer, Mrs Kapa."

Now Mrs Kapa smiled. "Henrietta, you really must learn to control your temper in class. It gets you in trouble too much of the time."

Henrietta felt another burst of temper coming on right then.

Mrs Kapa went on. "Yes, Henrietta, you must learn to control your temper, but I'm not sure that writing lines is going to help you do it. You're obviously a good thinker. So the next time you feel a temper coming on, try to think before you explode."

Henrietta thought.

Henrietta smiled.

Henrietta walked over to her desk and sat down.

Does Becky Bite?

"Hank, Honey, run up to Barbara's, will you?"

"What for?"

"To feed Becky."

"Why doesn't Barbara do it?"

"She's gone fishing, and I said we'd do it."

"Why don't you send Henrietta?"

"Because Henrietta's already in bed— because I asked *you*, Hank."

"How about asking Dad?"

"Oh Hank Prank! Get a move on!"

And so it was that Hank Prank, alias Henry Bradley Lawes, started trudging up Ravensbourne Hill to feed Becky.

Becky was big and black and curly. She was a bit poodley, a little collieish and a trifle Labradorian, but mainly she was big and black and curly. She had large, shiny white teeth which showed when she smiled, and she smiled and twirled her long black tail like a propeller whenever one of her friends came for a visit. And Hank was certainly one of her friends.

Hank heard his mother call after him as he started up the hill, "Becky's on the porch, and the food's in the fridge. Don't forget to give her some water."

"I won't, Mom."

"And the lightswitch is just inside the porch door. Don't you want to take your flashlight, Hank?"

"Naa, I don't need it." And he continued up the hill.

Hank wasn't quite sure he didn't need his flashlight, but he was quite sure it wouldn't do him any good if he did need it. Last night he'd used it to make shadow pictures on his bedroom wall, and when he woke up this morning, the switch was still on and the batteries were f-l-a-t.

So now Hank was walking to Barbara's house in the dark. In fact, he noticed that this night was especially dark. There was no moon, and by the time he got to. Barbara's, there were no more street lights either.

A cold whisper of wind came rushing down the hill, and Hank shivered as it brushed by him. I'll just let Becky know it's me, he thought. "Becky! Becky! It's me, Hank."

Becky didn't answer.

Hank stopped. Barbara's house was dark. He called again. "Becky! It's Hank, Becky. Are you there, Beck?"

Becky didn't answer.

Hank took a couple of steps, then stopped again. "Becky! Becky! Where are you, girl?"

Becky didn't answer.

Hank took another step. He was almost to the porch. Becky was on the porch. So why wasn't Becky answering? Just one little friendly woof would be enough. She always woofed when Barbara was home.

But Barbara wasn't home. Maybe Becky's guarding the house until she gets back . . . Maybe she's a guard dog . . . Maybe she's a trained attack dog . . . Maybe she's a *natural* attack dog . . . Maybe . . . Hank called again. This time he could hear a shaky-quaky sound in his voice.

"B-becky! B-becky! It's your friend, Hank. I've come to feed you. Nice doggy. N-nice . . ."

Hank made himself take one more step. He was just outside the porch door now. Becky was probably just inside it. It was dark, very dark. The porch was as black as . . . as black as . . . Becky. How was he going to see her?

The lightswitch! Where did Mom say it was? Just inside the door. So all I have to do is open the door a little, reach my arm in, and turn on the light. That's all I have to do. I'll hold the door with my other hand so Becky can't rush out and . . . and . . .

Hank didn't want to think about what Becky might do. He reached out for the door knob and was just about to turn it when he remembered something. He remembered something awful. What Hank remembered was Becky's big, shiny, white pointy teeth. Henry Bradley Lawes, alias Hank Prank, gulped. If he stuck his little arm in and Becky was lurking right behind the door . . . The picture of what might happen came flooding over him like a horror movie:

A sudden movement. Black dog. Wild eyes. Flashing white points. A horrible snap. YARGGH!

"Becky! Becky! Answer me, Becky! *Please*, Becky. Please answer."

Becky didn't answer.

"Then please, oh please, don't eat my arm off."

With his left hand, Hank s-l-o-w-l-y turned the knob. S-l-o-w-l-y, he opened the door, just wide enough to let his right arm *in* and not wide enough to let a mad, vicious, natural attack dog with razor fangs *out*. He forced his poor right arm through the opening. And waited for the bite.

Hank's frightened fingers fumbled

furiously for the lightswitch. They couldn't find it. Hank wished he had his flashlight. He wished he had on a leather jacket. He wished he had on a suit of armour. He tried not to, but he snorfulled a bit when he couldn't find the switch. He had a horrible feeling that Becky was about to have her first taste of arm sandwich.

Hank's hand bumped into something hard. It was the lightswitch! He breathed out and realized that he hadn't breathed at all for a long time. With quivering fingers, Hank switched on the porch light. He opened the door a crack wider. No Becky.

She wasn't lurking by the door. He opened it a little wider. She wasn't in front of the door. He opened it a lot wider and stuck his head in. She wasn't waiting to pounce on him from behind the door. Hank stepped onto the lighted porch. Becky wasn't anywhere! He breathed again.

"Becky! C'mon, girl, where are you?"

Suddenly, Hank heard a small whimper from the far side of the porch. He looked, and looked again. He couldn't believe his eyes. There in the furthest corner, hiding under a table, trying not to move at all but trembling with fear from her nose to her tail—cowered Becky.

"Becky!" Hank nearly cried with relief.

"Becky, you big silly! You're scareder of me than I was of you! You're still shaking even with the light on. Oh, Becky!"

Hank rushed over to her and threw his arms around her curly, black neck. "It's OK, Beck. Don't be afraid. It's only me. It's your friend, Hank Prank."

Becky stopped trembling. She licked Hank's face, she smiled her shiny white smile and twirled her long black tail like a propeller.

Tensions Rising

When the Lawes family finally decided that they were going to take their vacation at Lake Wobegon, everyone agreed it was a great idea. And when they belted themselves into the car at 9.30 on a clear summer morning, the only grumble was a brief and quiet one from Mr Lawes: "We were *supposed* to be on the road by 8.30."

But no one really cared, and because the day was fine and traffic was light, even he soon forgot about his schedule. By noon they were in the mountains where they all had the same instant reaction to the smell of pine— the four Lawes' stomachs began growling like bears at the same time.

Mr Lawes almost always tried to get just a little bit further, to drive just a few more miles to the next restaurant or petrol station, but this time he glanced only once at his watch and pulled into the very next restaurant they came to.

Henrietta and Hank rushed ahead to the toilets so they would have some extra time to study the moose head hanging on the wall. Mr and Mrs Lawes stretched, breathed deeply in the mountain air, and strolled into the restaurant arm-in-arm.

After lunch Hank and Henrietta had no trouble convincing their parents that they should all take a short hike through the pines to see the waterfall. Well, the hike turned out to be short-ish rather than short, and the time they spent barefoot in the stream turned out to be long-ish rather than short, and the ten minutes they wasted searching for Henrietta's Swiss Army knife turned out to be completely unnecessary when she finally remembered that she'd left it at home on her bed. By the time they hiked back to the car, they were another hour behind Mr Lawes' schedule.

It was just as they were pulling out of the parking lot that Hank realized he had to pee.

"I gotta pee," he announced.

"You did that before we ate," his father answered.

"Yep. I peed then and now I gotta pee again."

"Hank, couldn't you hold it for a while? We're already behind schedule."

Mrs Lawes looked disapprovingly at her husband. "Marc!" was all she said.

Mr Lawes stopped the car. Hank unbuckled his seatbelt, opened the door, climbed out, and disappeared into the restaurant. It was exactly seven minutes later by his father's very accurate watch that he returned.

"What on earth were you doing all that time?"

"I was talking to the moose." Hank slid into the back seat and buckled himself in.

"Talking to the *moose*?" Everybody laughed except Mr Lawes, who muttered something about that prankish kid and sped the car on to the highway.

They hadn't gone five miles when from the

back seat, Henrietta's small voice said, "I feel sick."

Her father kept driving. Then Henrietta's normal voice called, "Daddy, I feel sick."

Her father kept driving. *Then*, Henrietta's BIG voice boomed in her father's ears, "STOP THIS STUPID CAR I'M GONNA THROW UP AND I MEAN IT!"

Her kind, considerate father stopped the car. He pulled off to the side of the road by a meadow where Hank tried to interest a bored horse in a handful of grass while Henrietta paced back and forth looking ill. The horse didn't move, and Henrietta wasn't sick. But she kept pacing and kept looking awful.

"I told you she shouldn't have drunk that second milkshake," Mr Lawes snapped at his wife.

"You told *me*? *You* were the one who ordered it!"

Henrietta paced some more, but despite a huge overload of chocolate milkshake, she never did throw up. Eventually they climbed back into the car, parents in front, kids in the back, and all in a stew. Mr Lawes decided to make up time and pushed the accelerator a little harder than usual. On the dashboard, the speedometer needle glided up to the speed limit and then tiptoed past it. Mrs Lawes tried not to notice, but from where she was sitting it was impossible not to see the needle climb. She watched and worried as it pointed menacingly at her. She thought: if I say anything, it's only going to make his mood worse, and we'll end up having a fight in front of the kids. So I won't say a word.

And she didn't. For almost three minutes. Then she thought: but if I *don't* say anything, he'll drive even faster, and we'll crash into a telegraph pole. So I'll think of a kind and clever way to call our excessive speed to Marc's attention.

And she nearly did. But *then* she thought: why am I so worried about his precious feelings when this maniac is gonna get us killed? What's the matter with me?

So Mrs Lawes didn't say nothing. And she didn't say, "Darling, there may be a speed-trap around the next bend." What she *did* say was, "Stop this car this minute, you big blockhead!"

Her husband's face looked surprised and hurt. "Thank you very much, Dora. Maybe you'd like to drive if you don't like the way—"

"Yes, as a matter of fact I would. Stop the bloomin' car!"

He pulled over once again, and they changed places in silence. Their silence grew louder as the drive continued, with Mrs Lawes carefully driving five miles-an-hour *slower* than the speed limit, and Mr Lawes glaring at his watch. Neither of them said one word.

The silence was awful.

Now, if there was one thing Hank and Henrietta hated, it was when their parents had a fight. And they hated the silent ones worst of all. But they'd found a way to deal with it. Whenever Mr and Mrs Lawes had one of their silent fights—Hank and Henrietta had one of their noisy ones. This time, Henrietta made the first move. "Hey, shove over! You're on my side."

"I am not."

"Hank, move *over*! You're on my side."

"How can I be on your side, Dumbo, when I'm wearing this seatbelt?"

"Your foot is on my side, and you're the Dumbo. You should hear what Natalie says about you."

"Who cares what dumb old Natalie says about anything?"

"You do, 'cause *you* think she has 'bootifull blue eyes'. And you're so dumb you can't even spell 'beautiful'. Nyaah!"

That was the quiet, dignified part of their fight. The noisy, immature part was about to begin. At exactly the same moment Hank *and* Henrietta screamed in their parents' ears:

"Ma, she's been readin' my Secret Book!"

"Daddy, that little pig is making fun of my best friend!"

Then they hollered (also at the same time),

"You're the pig, you snoutnose hog!"

"You're a horrible, monstermouth brat!"

Then they started to pummel each other and pull each other's hair and cause one another bodily harm, at least as much as two kids who are seat-belted-in can pummel and pull and cause, which isn't a lot, but which sounds like they're bashing each other's brains out.

And just as suddenly as the back seat erupted into this furious chicken fight, so did the silence in the front seat explode and disappear. With her eyes in the rear-view mirror, Mrs Lawes called loudly to the top of the steering wheel, "Children, that is dangerous, and you know it. You could cause an accident with that kind of behaviour. You must not distract the driver from the—"

Mr Lawes whirled around in his seat and made a grab for his squabbling kids. But he forgot about his seatbelt. As he rose up out of his seat, the belt sprang into action and *whumped* him back down into it. He struggled a second time to turn as far as the belt would allow, gave his pummelling, hairpulling children a furious stare (as furious as a father who's just been pinned by a seatbelt could), and bellowed "You two cut that out and I'M NOT KIDDING!"

They cut it out.

Another Lawes family fight was over.

And they drove

Hotly,

Prankishly,

S-l-o-w-l-y,

On

To Lake Wobegon.

74

Sleigh Bawls
in the Snow

As a special, special winter treat, Hank Prank and his class were going on an old-fashioned sleigh ride. Miss Wiegand said, "Remember, kids, don't come to school tomorrow. We'll meet at nine o'clock at the Perry farm in Brownington Village."

The next morning, well before daylight, Hank appeared in his parents' room. He was dressed in a snowsuit, mittens, galoshes, and red ski hat with a pom-pom dangling from the top. "Sleigh ride day! Sleigh ride day!" he shouted as he pulled the quilt off their bed.

"Ey AHH! What's going on?" his father called, diving for the quilt. But Hank was too quick for him. He whisked the cover out of his father's freezing fingers.

"Come on, Hank. Give us a break. It's not even light out yet," his mother moaned, trying to snuggle up to her husband who was by now sitting and shivering with the sheet wrapped around him.

"Sleigh ride," Hank repeated. "Everybody up for the sleigh ride!"

And he disappeared out the door and down the stairs with the quilt trailing behind him.

"One day that kid is gonna go too far," Mr Lawes muttered as he groped for his long underwear.

"Little Hank goes too far *every* day," mumbled Mrs Lawes, still groping for something to cuddle. From downstairs they could hear Hank banging on a pot with a wooden spoon.

Henrietta appeared in her jammies at their bedroom door, sleepily holding her blankey to her cheek. "Whazamadda?" she asked.

"Nothing, Honey. Just go back to bed. It's too early for anybody to be up."

Soon the Lawes family, minus Henrietta, was in the kitchen. Hank was talking non-stop about horses and sleighs while his parents tried to get breakfast without opening their eyes.

At exactly 8.30 a.m. Hank hopped into the cold car and picked up the window scraper. While his mother warmed up the engine, Hank hopped out again and went around the windows scraping off the layer of new snow which had fallen during the night. They belted themselves in and drove slowly over to Brownington, then down a snowy lane to the Perry place. Hank said dreamily, "Wait'll we see those horses!"

His mother answered, "Now, Henry, you be sure and listen to Miss Wiegand."

When they arrived, other kids and their parents were stomping around in the snow and chattering excitedly outside Perry's barn. Miss Wiegand was there too. She trudged over as Mrs Lawes hopped out of the car. "Hi, Hank. Hi, Dora," she called.

"Good morning, Miss Wiegand. You're very brave, taking this lot out in the snow."

"Where are the horses?" asked Hank.

Just as he spoke, there came from the barn the sound of jingling bells. Around the corner of the building, a pair of thick-coated work horses, puffing steam into the cold morning air, trotted heavily through the snow. They looked a hundred feet tall. All the foot stamping and chatter stopped as kids and parents silently watched Mr Perry guide the team to a long logging sleigh covered with hay. With a click of his tongue and a flick of his switch, he backed the big horses into place while his son Dean hitched them to the sleigh.

There was a sudden mass movement. Every kid at the same time leapt on to the

sleigh and dived, head first, into and under
and through the hay. Dean hopped on too
while his father climbed into the driver's seat.
Miss Wiegand spoke to the bits of hat and
mitten and sleeve that poked through the
moving pile of hay. "Now children. I want
you to have fun today, and I also want you to
sit *away* from the sides of the sleigh. We don't
want anyone bouncing off into the snow."
And with that she hoisted herself onto the
sleigh and sat in the hay next to Dean. Mr
Perry clicked his tongue, the team strained at
their harnesses, and they were off.

"Goodbye! Goodbye! Be careful! Listen to
Miss Wiegand!" the parents called to the hay
pile.

The hay pile answered with a song—
"A hundred bottles of beer on the wall,
  A hundred bottles of beer . . ."
The team of horses pulled sleigh, hay, and kids through woods and snowy fields. They followed logging trails that they and Mr Perry knew well. When the singing stopped, heads popped out of the hay to see where they were and where they were going. One of the heads belonged to Henry Bradley Lawes, alias Hank Prank. Hank didn't want to see where they were going—he wanted to see where they'd been.

So he clambered to the rear of the sleigh and watched the trees go by. To get a better view, he dangled his legs over the back. Hank might have remembered Miss Wiegand's words, but now he wanted to see what kind of tracks the runners made in the snow. To get an even better look, Hank leaned over and peered down through his legs. At that very moment the sleigh hit a bump in the trail. The bump was just big enough to *plunk* Hank off the sleigh and *whunk* him into the snow.

Hank landed on his bottom, but he was so surprised to find himself sitting in the snow instead of sitting in the hay, that for a minute he couldn't even speak. When his voice found him again, he called out, "Hey, wait for me!" But the sleigh was already gone. He could just hear the bells jangling further and further away from where he sat.

Hank sat there in the snow. Hank thought there in the snow. Here's what Hank thought . . .

They've gone. I'm all by myself. Alone. Well, so what! Who needs 'em, anyway. I'm happy to be here in the woods just sitting by myself with nobody around except for the birds and the chipmunks and the deer and *maybe a bear*.

But I'm not afraid. I'll just whistle.

He tried to whistle, but his lips were too cold to pucker. All that came out was, "Whoo Whoo."

I'm not gonna whistle. I'm gonna sing. Hank cleared his throat. "Harrumph." He opened his mouth. "Aaahh."

He sang as loud as he could:

"A hundred bottles of beer on the wall.

A hundred bottles of . . ."

A tear squeezed its way out of Hank's left eye. Another tear snuck down from Hank's right eye. Hank's mouth was still singing, but no words were coming out. What did come out wasn't a word but something that sounded like this:

Wwwwaaaaahhaaaaahhaaahhahahhahahhhh!!!

80

It sounded like a firetruck with a sore throat. It was so loud it would have scared any bear that wasn't sleeping. It was so loud it would have scared any bear that *was* sleeping. It was so loud that Hank never even heard the clomping of horses' hooves in the snow or jangling bells coming closer and closer.

Hank's sore throat-siren ground down, but before he could catch his breath to start it again, he got a feeling that someone or some *thing* was watching him. *Bears?* He s-l-o-w-l-y turned around. Just in front of him, in the middle of the trail, stood four treetrunks. Four *hairy* treetrunks. Hank looked down.

The hairy trunks had horse hooves attached to their bottoms. Hank looked up. The hairy treetrunks had horse heads attached to their tops. The horses' big, curious eyes gazed down at Hank through the steam that snorted from their nostrils.

Miss Wiegand came running from behind them, knelt in the snow, and held Hank in her arms. "Don't cry, Henry," she said.

Hank snorfulled. "Cry? Me, cry? Why should I cry?"

"Well, I thought you might be afraid, all alone here in the snow."

"Miss Wiegand, please. I, Henry Bradley Lawes, don't know the meaning of fear. Besides, what is there to be afraid of?"

"Bears, Hank?"

"Bears, Miss Wiegand?"

"Bears, Hank."

"Oh. Bears. Well, yes, I might be afraid of bears, if there were any, but as there aren't, I'd be perfectly happy to continue to sit here by myself enjoying the snow."

Miss Wiegand took her arms from around Hank and looked at him thoughtfully. Suddenly Hank began to think what she might say. She might say, "OK, Henry, you stay here, and we'll leave you alone." Hank started to snorful again.

Finally Miss Wiegand spoke. She said,

"Wouldn't you rather come back to school for some hot chocolate?"

One more tear slipped out of each of Hank's eyes. "Well," he answered, "I sure do like hot chocolate."

A Room
of her Own

"You must clean up that room of yours, Henrietta! I was just up there and it looks like a pigsty."

"Mom, you said I didn't have to."

"I never said that, Henrietta. When did I say that?"

"You said it was my room, and I could do anything I wanted with it."

"I meant you could *decorate* it any way you wanted, not turn it into the town junkyard."

"I can decorate it any way I want?"

"Uh, yes."

"Well, what you call 'junkyard' is what I call 'decorate'."

"What?"

"And since it's my room, I think I ought to be the one who decides what's junk and what's . . . what's . . ."

"Decoration, Henrietta?"

"No, I'm trying to think of a better word."

"Art? Not 'art', Henrietta. Surely, not art."

"No, a better word."

"Wallpaper?"

"No, it's more like 'art'."

"Uh, let me think. Found objects?"

"I know! *Style!* Since it's my room, I'm the one who should decide what's junk, and what's . . . style."

"Henrietta, you ought to be a lawyer."

"Maybe I will."

"Or a union negotiator."

"What's a negotiator? Is it like a gladiator?"

"No, and it's not like a radiator. A negotiator is someone who's paid to argue, and since you argue so well—and so often— maybe you should earn your living that way."

"No, thanks. I'm going to be a vet."

"Good. You can argue with the cows. But in the meantime, let's go and inspect that junkyard—I mean, that sty-le you live in. Sty-le—get it, Henrietta?"

"I get it, Mom, I get it."

"If you get it, why didn't you laugh?"

"Maybe it was . . . boaring."

"Ooh, Henrietta. Child, I think you'd be wasted on cows. To your room!"

Up the stairs they marched, but before entering the room, they stopped outside the door. Henrietta's mother sighed. "This is a door? Henrietta, this is—"

"Style."
Together, they gazed at the door.
Here's what they saw.

"Henrietta, this isn't a door, it's an artefact."

"I said it was art, didn't I?"

"An artefact isn't the same as art. An
artefact is something archeologists dig out of a
hole in the ground."

"Why?"

"Why, what?"

"Why do artyologists dig arty facts out of a hole in the ground?"

"So they can tell about what kind of people lived there. You know, what kind of paintings they liked, what they made their pots out of—that kind of thing."

"Mom, if artyologists ever dug up my door—or my room—do you know what they'd call the people who lived here?"

"No, Henrietta, what would archeologists call you?"

"They'd call me 'stylish'."

"Do you know what I call you?"

"Junkyard?"

"No, I call you Hot Henrietta, the world's best arguer."

"Does that mean we don't have to inspect my room?"

"Let's go down to the kitchen, Henrietta. I could do with some hot chocolate."

Song of Songs

"Eye tiddly eye-tie,
Eat brown bread.
I saw a sausage
Fall down dead.
Up jumped a saveloy
And thumped him
On the head.
Eye tiddly eye-tie,
Brown bread."

From where Mr Lawes sat in the driver's seat, the noise was deafening, but from where Hank and Henrietta and Ben and Toby sat in the back, their singing was just plain wonderful. As they finished the thirteenth chorus of 'Brown Bread', Mr Lawes made the mistake of saying, "That was lovely, kids. Now why don't you do something else, like play 'Teacher'." The four friends immediately swung into the song about the teacher.

"On top of Old Smokey,
  All covered with sand,
  I shot my poor teacher,
  With a big rubber band.
  I shot her with pleasure,
  I shot her with pride,
  I just couldn't miss her,
  She was forty feet wide.
  I went to her funeral,
  I wept at her grave,
  Some people threw flowers,
  I threw a grenade."

That one was good for seven choruses. By the seventh, Mr Lawes was trying desperately to think of a way to stop the music. "That's an old tune, kids. I bet your mother and father know it, Ben and Toby. We used to sing it when we were your age. It's called 'On Top of Old Smokey'. Some day we'll have to sing it to—"

Without another moment's hesitation, the back seat broke into another version of the song. It went like this:

"On top of spaghetti,
  All covered with cheese,
  I lost my poor meatball,
  When somebody sneezed.
  It rolled off the table,
  And on to the floor,

And then my poor meatball,
Rolled out of the door . . ."

"Kids, that's enough."
But that wasn't enough. That was just the
end of the first verse.

"It rolled through the garden,
And under a bush,
And then my poor meatball,
Was nothing but mush."

"OK, kids, that's enough, now. We're
gonna have *five* minutes of *silencio*."
But the song *still* wasn't over.

"So when you eat spaghetti,
All covered in cheese.
Hold on to your meatball,
If somebody sneezes."

When it came time to rhyme 'cheese' and 'sneezes', the four friends fell about with laughter. In fact, they rolled onto the floor just like their poor meatball. And their laughter was nearly as loud as their singing.

"Hey, I can't see you guys in the mirror. C'mon. Get up! Where are those meatbelts—I mean seatbelts?"

Henrietta covered her grinning mouth with her left hand, and waved two fingers of her right in the rear-view mirror. More giggling.

"Oh, yeah. There are four of you and only two belts."

For some reason, this instantly convulsed the four of them into even more laughter. The whole car shook. Mr Lawes wished he could take his hands off the steering wheel and hold them over his ears.

"Look, let's have a little quiet, just long enough for my ears to stop ringing. If it lasts long enough, maybe I'll get you some ice-cream on the—"

> "Row, row, row your boat,
> Gently down the stream.
> Steal your teacher's pocketbook,
> And fill it full of cream!"

"Children! Ben! Toby! Henrietta! Hank-for-goodness-sake! I'm talking to you. *I need some silence!*"

There was some silence.

From the front seat, Mr Lawes muttered under his breath, "Hallelujah."

Instantly, the Back Seat Chorus shouted,

"Glory, glory hallelujah,
Teacher hit me with a ruler,
Father hit me with a walking stick,
Till I was black and blue."

"Enough! Enough! All right, it's over."

But only the first verse was over. The second verse was about to begin.

"Glory, glory hallelujah,
Teacher hit me with a ruler,"

"Kids, you already sang that—"

"I hid behind the door,
With a Magnum forty-four,
And my teacher lived no more."

"Very funny, I'm sure. Now will the four of you—"

"Glory, glory hallelujah,"

"Oh, no!"

"Teacher hit me with a ruler,"

"Not again!"

"I hit her on the bean,"

"My eardrums are bursting!"

"With a rotten tangerine,"

"Mercy! Please, I beg you."

"And her teeth came marching out."

This song continued despite increasingly feeble protests from the driver. Finally, the last verse ended with the beautiful refrain,

"And her brains rolled out the door."

The final chorus rolled through the driver's brain like a bowling ball crashing through a stack of tin cans. His head hurt. His ears clanged. And he was downright disgusted that all his begging and pleading and bribing and arguing were having no effect whatsoever on the volume of horrible songs from the boresome foursome. They had miles to go before home, and he felt like his poor ears would collapse before they got there. Even now he could see through the rear-view mirror that the fiendish four were catching their breaths and whispering about the next selection.

Then he had an idea. Quietly, but very quickly, before the next kids' song began, he started one of his own. Here's how it went . . .

"Yea-boo, yea-boo,
Lots of fun to do,

If you like it holler 'yea!',
If you don't you holler 'boo!'"

Then he sang,

"There's a tavern in the town . . ."
There was a longish silence, a longish puzzled silence, from the back seat. Finally, Henrietta, in an unsure voice, answered, "Yea?"

"But the cops have shut it down."
Henrietta and Ben both responded with a "Boo".

"It will open up tonight . . ."
Three "yea's" from behind.

"Without a single drink in sight."
Four decisive "boo's".

"All the sandwiches are free . . ."
"Yea."

"For everyone but you and me."
"Boo."
Mr Lawes sang another chorus,

"Yea-boo, yea-boo,
Lots of fun to do,
If you like it holler 'yea!',
If you don't you holler 'boo!'"

And added,

"There's no drinking!"
"Boo."
"Only champagne!"

"Yea."

"No glasses."

"Boo."

"Buckets!"

"Yea."

"The buckets have holes in 'em."

"Boo."

"Holes are on the top."

"Yea."

"Only three dancing girls."

"Boo."

"Two dresses . . ."

"YEA!" (especially from Ben and Toby)

"To each girl."

"Boo!"

"But they're made of Cellophane!"

"YEA! YEA!"

"You can't take 'em with you."

"Boo."

"THEY TAKE *YOU*!"

"YEA! YEA! YEA!"

Then they all sang a chorus together.

"Yea-boo, yea-boo,
  Lots of fun to do,
  If you like it holler 'yea!',
  If you don't you holler 'boo!'"

The five of them were still singing when they pulled into Ben and Toby's driveway.

Their mother, Penny, was waiting for them as the car rolled to a stop.

"How was the trip, Marc?"

"Now, let's see, Penny, how shall I describe it? Ben, Toby, Henrietta, Hank—would I be fair to describe it as . . . harmonious?"

The 'Glorious Fourofus' answered with one voice:

"YEA! ! !"